Baby, Don't Go

Yeah, Baby 3

FIONA DAVENPORT

Copyright

*The pregnancy might
be accidental, but
their love is not.*

Chapter 1

JACK

"Hey, Ellie!" I yelled as I jogged down the sterile halls of the hospital. A white lab coat and dark brown ponytail had just disappeared around the corner. As I reached the turn, I rammed into said lab coat and ponytail, knocking us both to the ground. I caught her as we fell, so that she landed on top of me. Soft tits were pressed against my chest, wisps of straight, toffee-colored hair tickled my chin, and a sweet, elfin face grinned at me, while her hazel eyes danced with amusement.

"You're pretty clumsy for a surgeon, honey," she laughed, then lightly smacked my shoulder. "And, would you stop calling me Ellie?"

The endearment brought warmth to my chest and her laugh started a buzz in the general area of my dick. I shoved both feelings away. Ellison Reed was my friend. In fact, since my best friend had gone and knocked up, then married my sister, Ellie (no, I wouldn't stop calling her that) had basically taken his place.

She jumped to her feet and I followed, my own grin splitting my face. "I don't know what you're talking about, Dr. Reed. You plowed into me.

Ellison snorted, "You wish."

Yes. I did wish, but I wasn't about to admit it aloud. I raised a single eyebrow. "You think so?"

She shook her head. "Well, since your blow-up girlfriend deflated..."

I tweaked her nose. "Funny, funny girl."

Winking at me, she curtseyed. "Thank you."

Damn, she was adorable. Or, you know, cute. Like a friend. "Alright, Dr. Comedienne, I have a surgery in half an hour, but I wanted to see if we were still on for movie night at my place."

"Yep. My last case should be done by five, so I'll grab a shower and pick up Chinese on the way. I should be there by six."

"Great. And none of that all vegetable crap you got last time. I'm a growing boy, I need meat, woman!" Her short ponytail was swinging and I couldn't resist tugging it before I walked away, her laughter following me, bringing back those damn tingles.

Ellison and I had worked together on and off over the last two years. She was a general pediatric surgeon and when her patients needed a specialist in pediatric vascular surgery, she usually requested me. However, a few months ago, we ran into a tough case and ended up working long hours together. We began to realize we had a lot in common, a love of crappy horror movies, Thai food, eighties music, and baseball. When Wyatt, had to cancel a baseball game with me, I invited Ellison. From there, things took off and we'd been inseparable ever since.

I'd always been attracted to her, but the friendship we'd developed was important to me and I decided never to cross the line out of the "friend zone." Friday nights became movie night for us most weeks and I was looking forward to unwinding with her, a cold beer, and a shitty B-list horror film.

My afternoon was spent with a tough case, and by the time the surgery was done, I was strung tight with stress and worry.

"I want updates every hour for the next four hours," I told my nurse as I finished writing Heather's orders. She was only six years old and in critical condition. "Then I want another update every four hours from then on."

"No problem, Dr. Halston." She finished hooking up Heather's IV and followed me from the small room in the ICU, both of us stopping at the nurse's station to drop off paperwork.

I changed into street clothes in the locker room and tossed my scrubs in a laundry bin on my way out the door. Entering the employee-parking garage, I strolled over to my Mercedes convertible and popped the remote lock. Getting in, I put down the top and drove out into the balmy, summer evening. On the way home, I stopped by the store for beer and a carton of Moose Tracks, Ellison's favorite ice cream. When I arrived at my house, I pulled into the four-car garage and parked next to my Ducati. Taking everything inside, I put the groceries away and hopped in the shower, washing away the grime and some of the stress from the day. Afterwards, I dressed in an old pair of comfy jeans and a grey T-shirt, but stayed barefoot, enjoying the feel of my soft, plush carpet on my feet.

I pulled my comforter off of the bed and took it to the couch, knowing Ellie would get cold and ask me for it eventually anyway, and tossed it onto one of the couches in my theater room. I checked my phone for an update on my patient and was pleased to know she was improving. When the doorbell rang, I walked down the hall and into my large entryway, to the front door and twisted the handle. Opening it, I found Ellison holding plastic bags in one hand and munching on an egg roll with the other. Her plump lips closed around the cylindrical food and I fought a groan as I suddenly pictured those plump lips around a similarly shaped part of my body. *You need to get laid, dude.* Clearly, six months of celibacy had put my fucking hormones into overdrive. It didn't help matters to see her wearing yoga pants that molded to her very fine legs and ass, and a large T-shirt that hung off one shoulder, revealing a bright purple bra strap.

"That better not be my egg roll," I growled playfully. Her eyes widened with innocent shock as she took another bite.

"You wanted one?" She popped the last of the greasy treat into her mouth and chewed slowly. I rolled my eyes and stood back, allowing her to enter.

"I saved you all of the crab rangoons, though," she tossed over her shoulder.

I felt my face screw up in a disgusted grimace, I hated seafood. "Hardy har, Ellie. Now, give me my food."

She set the bags on the table while I grabbed plates and silverware, bringing them over to her. We dished up our food, I grumbled over the vegetable fried rice and lo mein, and then we each grabbed a beer and headed for my theater room, settling on a couch to watch our movie. Ellie finished off two plates of food and I wondered, not for the first time, where she put all of it. She was barely five foot three and no more than one hundred and ten pounds, soaking wet. An image I've pictured a million times. I grabbed our plates, taking them to the kitchen and returning to find she'd taken over my couch. As usual.

She was wrapped up in the blanket I'd left for her and I lifted her mummified feet, so I could sit back on my end of the couch and let them drop into my lap. They were dangerously close to my cock and he had definitely taken notice. I focused on the movie, determined to forget about her sexy body and the proximity of her cute little feet to my budding erection. At one point, she ran a toe up her opposite leg, likely scratching it, but it was sexy as hell, and I had to clench my fists in order to keep from following the path of her foot with my hands. Then she shifted and when she brushed against my hard as fuck cock, I almost came in my pants right then and there. If she noticed the bulge in my crotch, she didn't mention it and I wasn't going to bring it up. All in all, it was fucking agony.

I managed to get through it, but when the credits started to roll, I jumped up, almost knocking her to the ground.

"Hey!" she yelped as she caught herself.

"Sorry, I need some...um...ice cream!" I hurried to the kitchen and opened the freezer, basking in the cool air. I dished up the bowls and returned to the living room, handing hers over and taking a seat in my black, leather recliner.

"Ready for the sequel?" I asked as I cued up the DVR.

She licked her spoon and let out a tiny little moan of delight. *Fuck!* Ok, stupid choice of words.

"Sure. Although, I'm not sure I'll be able to stay for it all."

I glanced at her in surprise. "You know you can crash here if it gets too late or if you want to have a couple of beers."

She nodded absentmindedly, continuing to dig into her ice cream, searching out the little peanut butter cups. "Yeah, I know. It's not that. I have an early date tomorrow."

Something inside me started to burn, an irrational anger building. Her *date* was cutting into my time with her, the bastard.

"What kind of a date happens on Saturday morning?" I muttered rhetorically.

"He's taking me horseback riding and wants to get an early start before it gets really hot." She didn't seem particularly enthusiastic about the date and it soothed a little of my ire. Why was I mad? What the fuck was wrong with me? I was being ridiculous.

"Sounds like he's a pretentious snob, showing off."

Ellison laughed at my comment, giving me a dry look. "Excuse me, but don't you own horses, Jack?"

"That's different," I huffed. "We're friends. I'd take you riding if you wanted to go. But, taking a woman horseback riding for a first date? What a tool."

It was Ellison's turn to roll her eyes and mutter, "What crawled up your ass tonight?"

"Nothing. I just think you shouldn't waste your time with losers and this guy is obviously trying to get in your pants by throwing his money in your face."

"What? Jack, seriously, what is wrong with you tonight?" Ellison stood and left the room. I followed at a slow pace, confused by my own behavior and having lost my appetite. I found her in the kitchen, loading all of our dishes into the dishwasher.

"I'm sorry," I mumbled. "Bad day, I guess."

She sighed. "Yeah. I'm going to head out."

I felt something akin to panic creeping into my chest. I couldn't let her walk out the door, because it would mean she'd be going on a date tomorrow morning. I couldn't let it happen, I just couldn't. I was stunned at my reaction and didn't know what to make of it. Before I was able to form a response, Ellison had left the room. I trotted to the entryway to find her grabbing her keys and cell phone from the glass bowl on the little marble table by the coat closet.

I stood there, watching, my arms hanging at my sides, not knowing what to do or say. She glanced at me with a half-smile as she slipped on her flip-flops and headed to the door.

I joined her and put my hand on it to keep it closed. "I'll see you Sunday for breakfast?" I asked tentatively.

"Oh, sorry. I forgot to tell you, he's taking me to a cabin by a lake for the night. That's why we want to get on the trail before the heat is unbearable."

"Your—um," I croaked as something began to choke me. "Your date is overnight? As in spending the night with him, in the cabin, alone?"

Ellison looked at me curiously. "Yes."

No. No fucking way in hell was that happening.

The tightness in my chest and throat snapped and a rush of adrenaline, lust, and uncontrollable need rushed through my body as though a dam had broken. My hand cupped the back of her neck, the other grasping her waist, and pulled her flush against my body, my mouth slamming down over hers.

Chapter 2

Ellison

I gasped in surprise as Jack's tongue slid inside my mouth. It tangled with mine as he devoured me, kissing me the way I'd always assumed he would on the rare occasions I allowed my thoughts to wander in that direction. Jack Halston was a sexy devil. I'd known it from the first moment I'd laid eyes on him, just as every woman did. At six foot two, with a toned body that showed he worked out during his off hours, dark hair that looked like he'd just rolled out of bed, and chocolate brown eyes that always seemed to be smiling, he was impossible to miss. At first, I was happy for him to be my work flirt when our paths crossed on a shared case. We didn't see each other often enough for it to be awkward, and I enjoyed the little thrill I got from the way we bantered back and forth.

Flirting with Jack offered me a naughty distraction, but I knew nothing would ever come of it. Jack had a rule about not sleeping with anyone from the hospital, a fact long bemoaned by the vast majority of the female staff who would have given just about anything to make him break it. There was no way I'd be the one to make him throw his rulebook out the window. When our friendship deepened a few months ago, the slim chance I ever had of seeing Jack naked became even less likely because we went from being work peers to friends. If a guy like Jack didn't sleep with his co-workers, then he most definitely didn't screw any of his female friends. A fact I'd reminded myself of each time I'd woken up from dreams about all the things I'd do to him if I ever had the chance.

I wasn't about to waste an opportunity like this. Shoving away all thoughts of what might happen to our friendship if this went sideways, I dropped my keys and phone back down and reveled in the feel of his lips over mine.

"Fuck it," he groaned into my mouth. "I'm done playing the nice guy, trying to ignore how hard you make me because you're my friend and co-worker. How you've made it fucking impossible for me to even look at another woman without comparing her to you."

Wait? Had his recent dry spell been because of *me*? Because I could definitely lay the blame for mine at his feet. It was hard to find a guy who measured up to my dreams of Jack. I'd finally talked myself into accepting this date with a guy who'd asked me about a dozen times whenever I bumped into him at the gym. The only reason I'd said yes was because I figured that at some point, I'd have to hear about Jack's dates with another woman.

"I'm not letting you walk out this door, knowing you'll be with some douchebag this weekend. He doesn't get to touch what's mine," he growled, making my pussy quiver at the possessiveness in his tone.

"And what exactly do you consider to be yours?" Yeah, that was my raspy voice, taunting him with my question when we both knew what he meant. I couldn't help myself. He'd started this, and I wanted to make sure he damn well finished it.

He crowded me closer to the door, his hard chest pressed against mine while his big hands held my hips. My heart raced as his lips traced a path along my cheek and up to my ear. His breath was hot as he answered my question, his fingers tightening on me. "You're mine."

"Oh, yeah?" I breathed. "Prove it, honey."

"I fucking love it when you call me honey." His voice was dark and dangerous, with none of the teasing quality that was always there between us. "And I can't fucking wait to taste yours."

His lips on me sounded like a great plan. "Yes, please."

"Looking at your curves without being able to touch them was pure torture." His hand drifted up from my hip, along the curve of my waist and my side until it rested below one of my tits. My nipples pebbled as his thumb swept upwards. His other hand tightened on my hip, holding me firmly against his cock while his hips flexed and pressed his length against me. "See what you do to me? I'm a walking hard-on whenever you're near."

"Maybe we should do something about that," I murmured, running my hands down his back, his muscles bunching underneath my fingertips.

"Not until I get my taste of you."

He dropped to his knees, shoving my yoga pants and panties down my legs and ripping them and my flip-flops off my body. He widened my stance and without warning, two fingers plunged into me. His thumb stayed on my clit, rubbing in circles.

I moaned, riding his hand as his fingers worked in and out of me, staring down at his dark head as his body flexed with each thrust of his fingers. All coherent thought flew out of my brain when he leaned forward and replaced his thumb with his lips at my clit. Alternating between sucking and licking, he never stopped thrusting his two fingers into me.

"I'm so close," I cried out, my body tightening when he sucked my clit hard and bit down gently. Intense pleasure ripped through my body, my hips jerking against him. He yanked his fingers out of me and slid his tongue as deep as it would go, fucking me through my orgasm as I rode his face.

He stood, keeping one hand on my waist to steady me. I was dazed from my climax, my eyes unable to focus on the sight of him fumbling with his zipper to free his cock.

"Tell me you want me inside you." He didn't wait for my answer, his lips crashing against mine once again. I tasted myself on him, our flavors mixed together. "Please, Ellie," he whispered against my mouth.

"Yes." My answer turned into a gasp when his hands grabbed the back of my thighs to pick me up. My legs wrapped around his hips, lining us up perfectly. He drove inside in one powerful thrust, my back slamming against the door.

He dropped his forehead onto mine, his brown eyes appearing even darker with desire. My pussy squeezed in response to the possessive gleam in them. My brain might not be sure exactly what was happening between us, but my body seemed more than okay to go with the flow and enjoy the ride.

"This first time, I know I should be gentle. I'm sorry I can't be," he groaned, grinding his hips into me and driving his cock even deeper. "I've waited too long and want you too much, but I swear I'll make it good for you, my Ellie."

"It's more than good just like this," I promised. "Take me, honey."

"So fucking perfect." His voice was rough against my neck as I wrapped my arms around his shoulders and tried moving my hips. His hold on me tightened further, to the point I was going to have bruises in the morning. Marks I'd wear proudly as a reminder of our night together.

He withdrew and then plunged back inside. Over and over again while he held me immobile against the wall and fucked me. Slowly at first and then his rhythm sped up, pushing me closer to the edge. I gasped each time he pounded into me, my cries ringing out between us.

"Come for me," he growled. "I need to feel your tight pussy strangling my cock."

I flew apart, moaning loudly as my body convulsed around him. My pussy fluttered, my legs tightening on his hips, and my arms clenching around his neck. My orgasm was huge. I swore I saw stars.

"Hottest thing I've ever seen," he groaned. "Just seeing you like that is enough to make me come, too."

His body shuddered as he proved his words to be true. He came hot and hard, deep inside me as he trembled. His hips pushed deeper, driving him further inside while his come filled me up and spilled down my thighs.

"Fuck," he hissed. "You feel so damn good, Ellie."

He felt better than good inside me. Of course he did. It wasn't just because we fit together perfectly, almost like his cock had been made to fill me. Nope, it felt beyond amazing because we'd done something I'd never done before. Jack had taken me bare. Without protection of any kind because I wasn't on birth control, hadn't been since I was a teenager and discovered I didn't react to the hormones well. We were doctors, for fuck's sake. We both knew the risks better than most people, and yet the thought of telling him to use a condom hadn't crossed my mind. Not once. *What the heck was up with that?*

Chapter 3

JACK

I had dreamed of fucking Ellison so many times, woken up in a cold sweat, on the verge of coming night after night. It didn't even come close to the real thing. I could barely breathe. My heart was pounding so hard, and while I felt sated from the relief of finally having her, it also fed my obsession. My cock was still hard as a rock, gloved in the heat of her pussy.

My hands moved from her hips to her plump, luscious ass and I quickly walked her to the back of the house and into my bedroom, not once losing our connection. Lowering her gently to the bed, I slipped out, her little mewl of protest hardening my cock even further, despite having just emptied myself into her. I tore my T-shirt over my head and dropped my jeans and boxers to the floor before joining her on the bed again. I helped her lift her shirt up and off, tossing it randomly because my eyes were glued to her tits, watching the full globes encased in purple silk rise and fall as she panted with arousal.

My hands slid up her sides, over her flat belly, and up to cup her tits. They filled my palms perfectly and I squeezed them, almost breaking at the sound of Ellison moaning. I reached one hand beneath her back and popped the clasp. The bra loosened and her tits spilled out, her dark pink nipples large and erect, begging for my mouth.

"You're fucking gorgeous, Ellie," I rumbled before taking one peak in my mouth. They tasted sweet, and I licked and sucked them like a fucking lollipop until Ellison was writhing, her fisted hands clutching the covers.

I could feel the sticky come between us and I decided to live out the fantasy of my woman soaking wet. In more ways than one. "Let's shower, baby."

She glared at me and I grinned and kissed her. "I promise it'll be the best fucking shower you've ever had."

She raised a single eyebrow and my smile widened. "Yeah, I definitely meant it both ways."

She laughed and I pulled her up off the bed, lifting her in my arms, to carry her to the bathroom while she clung to me, arms and legs locked around my body. I settled her on the counter and stepped inside my spacious, marble shower, turning on the water and waiting for it to heat to the perfect temperature.

Then I returned to her and picked her up, her body once again wrapping itself around me. I stepped under the spray and she groaned in pleasure.

"Ellie, baby, you keep making noises like that and you'll find yourself being fucked up against a second wall tonight."

"Promise?" she asked, her voice whisper soft, bathing the shell of my ear in her warm breath. I was tempted, so tempted, but there was something else I wanted more.

I lathered up my hands and washed her from head to toe, my control severely tested when she did the same to me. After rinsing, I grasped her waist and pulled her soft body into me.

"Now," I mumbled against her skin as I kissed my way down her body, "about your honey." I lowered to my knees and gasped at the glistening pink pussy on display. Rivulets of water ran down her legs and I had to know if the wetness was all from the shower. I parted her folds and immediately gave her one long, slow lick.

The taste of honey burst on my tongue and I growled before attacking her pussy. My tongue and teeth went to work, building my Ellie up until she was crying out.

I added two fingers to the mix and she screamed my name as she shattered. I jumped to my feet, spun her around, placed her hands on the wall, and thrust up into her pussy which was still pulsing with her orgasm. "Fuck, baby. You feel so good." I pulled her hips out a little and tilted her pussy, driving deeper before she could come down off of the ledge, and she was coming again. "I want another one, Ellie. Come on, baby. Take me deep." I thrust in harder and harder until I wrung a third orgasm from her and finally allowed myself to come. It rocked my fucking world.

After we had managed to catch our breath, I ran a hand from her hip down to cup her pussy. I felt a thick wetness leaking out and coating my fingers. Bringing my hand from between her legs, I stared at it covered in come.

What the fuck did I just do?

I'd taken Ellie bare. Twice. *Son of a bitch!*

We'd have to talk about it, but I needed time to process this, so I didn't say anything yet. She seemed to be in a haze, exhausted and sated. I fucking loved the look on her face. It brought the warmth back to my chest. I rinsed both of us and shut the water off before stepping out onto the heated tile. Grabbing two towels, I wrapped one around my waist, then gently dried Ellie off. Lifting her into my arms, I carried her to my big bed and helped her slide under the covers, before going around to the other side, climbing in, and pulling her into my arms. Her head rested on my shoulder and she sighed, gliding her hand over my stomach and up to rest on my sternum.

Holding her close, I contemplated our circumstances. From a previous conversation, I knew she wasn't on any type of birth control because of adverse reactions she'd experienced. I hadn't intended to act on the chemistry between us, but now that I had, there was no fucking way I was going to let her go. I wanted this, having her in my bed every night, forever. I pictured her walking down a flower covered aisle in a white dress and felt nothing but need and want, whereas I expected to be in a panic. The image morphed into a picture of Ellison with a swollen belly, her smile bright, and I was infused with excitement.

This could actually be the silver bullet. I wanted a family, especially after spending time with my sister, her husband, and their twins. I'd begun to seriously consider settling down. After giving in to my body's craving for Ellie, I realized I definitely wanted those things, but only with her. A baby would cement our commitment to each other. She was mine and everyone would know it.

The more I thought about it, the idea grew until I was determined to make it happen. Fuck the condoms, if Ellie wasn't already pregnant, I'd make damn sure she was as soon as possible. Getting her moved in right away was the first step to tackle. Set on a course of action, I fell asleep with a smile on my face and dreamt of my perfect future.

The next morning, I woke slowly, contentment washing over me as I ran my hands down the soft flesh of my woman wrapped up in my arms. She stirred and I looked down to see her eyes flutter then widen as her head popped up, looking around with something akin to panic in them. I frowned, frustrated that she apparently wasn't feeling the same level of satisfaction at waking up with me. She slowly went up onto an elbow and twisted to meet my gaze. The panic had eased, but it had been replaced with wariness.

"Good morning, beautiful," I purred, the back of my hand running down her cheek before pushing her hair back behind her ear. My words seemed to melt some of the wariness away and the tension in her shoulders lessened. She smiled at me, almost shyly, and it was so adorable I had to kiss her. Putting my hands on her torso, I hauled her up to press my lips to hers.

My morning hard-on was suddenly hard as a baseball bat and I scowled when she pulled back. She smiled again and I softened at the sight, wondering if she would always have the same effect on me.

"Morning," she whispered. She shifted and I saw a tiny wince, worrying me.

"Are you sore, baby? I probably shouldn't have taken you so hard last night."

Her cheeks became a sweet shade of pink. "Um, a little." She winked at me. "That battering ram you call a dick is larger than I'm used to." She mock glared at me. "Don't let that go to your head, honey. You have a hard enough time getting through doors as it is."

I laughed and enveloped her in a hug. I fucking loved her—what? I was glad she couldn't see my face at the moment. I'm sure I looked like a deer in headlights. Holy fuck. When had it happened? I was so in love with her. I just needed to make her fall in love with me, too. There was no other option.

"Why don't you hop in the shower, baby? I'll make us some breakfast."

She pouted at me, and I chortled. "If I take a shower with you, you'll be even more sore."

With a quick peck on her lips, I scooted to the edge of the bed and stood. Grabbing my cell phone, I checked my messages for news about Heather as I rooted around for my boxers and picked up all of our scattered clothes, throwing them in the hamper.

"Hey!" Ellie protested. "I don't have any other clothes here, honey."

I opened a drawer and tossed a T-shirt and clean boxers at her. She caught them and frowned. "I can't go home in these."

I raised an eyebrow. "Who said you were leaving?"

"I need to go home," she huffed.

I didn't reply until I was almost out the door then muttered loud enough for her to hear, "We'll see."

Chapter 4

Ellison

After a quick shower, I sniffed Jack's shirt, drawing the scent of his laundry detergent deep into my lungs, before pulling it over my head. Stepping into his boxers, I couldn't help but think I needed to detour to his laundry room to see what brand he used, so I could be surrounded by the smell every day. Then again, I wouldn't be able to do my job because I'd be distracted by memories of the night we'd spent together. I guessed that plan was out the window. If only my job literally wasn't life or death, the tradeoff might be worth it. Jack smelled *that* good.

I stopped in the foyer to grab my cell phone, unaccustomed to going more than a couple hours without checking it. Even when I wasn't on call, it wasn't rare for me to get calls with questions about my patients. A quick glance confirmed I'd only missed one call from the hospital, but they hadn't left a message so it must not have been urgent. As I heaved a sigh of relief, my phone rang with an incoming call—not from the hospital, but from my date. The one I'd completely forgotten about and had apparently stood up this morning, since I was supposed to have met him five minutes ago.

"Ellison Reed," I answered out of habit.

"I'm running a little late. Traffic was backed up because of an accident," Richard grumbled.

Some of my guilt evaporated at the irritation evident in his tone. I'd seen the results of too many accidents first-hand to ever feel anything but relieved my car wasn't involved and hopeful nobody was injured whenever I drove past one. Plus, as hypocritical as it was of me, I was a little bothered that he had waited until he was already late before calling me. I knew it was ridiculous, considering I was standing in the middle of Jack's house, dressed in his clothes after spending the night in his bed, but I was annoyed nonetheless.

"I'm sorry, Richard, but something's come up and I won't be able to make it today."

"Or any day," Jack growled in my ear, sneaking up on me and grinding his hips against my ass to demonstrate exactly what had come up. Again.

I shook my head to clear my thoughts, turning in his arms to press my palm against his mouth so he couldn't interrupt my call. Cancelling a date after it was supposed to have already begun was bad enough, I refused to do it with Jack whispering in my ear. Or even worse, not bothering to keep his voice down and making it clear to Richard exactly why I wasn't going to keep our date.

"I can't say I'm not disappointed, but I guess that's what happens when you're dating a successful surgeon. Do you think you'll be able to drive up later today or even tomorrow morning?"

Dating? How had my accepting one date with this guy turned into us dating? I should have realized he was going to turn into a Grade-A Clinger based on how many times he'd asked me out. Persistence wasn't always a good thing in a man, sometimes it was a sign of what's to come if you said yes.

"No, I won't be able to make it today or tomorrow."

Jack's eyes flared, and I felt his lips move against my skin. If the way his body tensed was any indication, he wasn't happy with the direction of my conversation with Richard, who was still jabbering off dates in my ear.

"Next weekend isn't good for me, either."

Jack's arms crossed over his chest while he leveled me with a glare. His eyebrow was quirked up in a challenging manner. We'd been friends long enough for me to know I didn't want him to decide he needed to take control of this discussion, not unless I wanted to switch gyms. And I liked my gym, dammit.

"As much as I appreciate your offer to reschedule, I probably shouldn't have taken you up on your offer in the first place, Richard."

"C'mon, Ellison. Don't back out now. It took me forever to get you to say yes in the first place. I'd hate to have to ask you another dozen times to hear you say it again."

Maybe Jack was right, and Richard really was a loser who wanted to get into my pants. A very persistent loser who might force me to switch gyms anyway. Why had I agreed to this date in the first place?

Oh, yeah. I returned Jack's glare with one of my own. I'd been caught in a weak moment while trying to convince myself I should date someone else because Jack was just my friend. Really, an argument could easily be made that this whole situation was his fault for not making a move sooner.

I dropped my hand away from his mouth and muttered into the phone, "Asking me another dozen times isn't going to change anything. I'm not going to meet you today and I won't be saying yes to you in the future."

"That's what you told me the fifth time I asked you out."

He'd kept track of my responses? I made a mental note to check out other gyms in the very near future. Avoiding the creepy guy I'd almost spent the day with was now a top priority for me. And night, gag!

"It's not going to happen, Richard. Not the next time you ask, or a dozen times after that. So do us both a favor and stop asking me."

I disconnected the call while he was in the middle of arguing with me. I'd clearly had a close call with him and he wasn't worth any more of my time, not when I had the object of my own obsession standing right in front of me—grinning, the smug bastard.

"It's a good thing you made it clear you weren't interested. There's only room for one dick in this relationship and it sure as hell isn't him."

"I'll have you know, Richard doesn't like to be called Dick," I countered, while doing a little dance in my head over the fact that Jack had just called whatever was happening between us a relationship.

He tugged on my arm, leading me into the living room and pulling me down so I was straddling his lap on the couch. "How about you worry about this dick instead," he murmured in my ear, grinding his hips upwards.

His hot length bumped against my clit, making me shudder. I twined my arms around his neck and pushed my knees into the cushions on either side of his hips as I moved over him. His hands slid under my shirt, skimming up my back. I circled my hips and his fingers dug into my skin. Then his lips were on mine, his tongue pushing into my mouth and exploring. One of his hands slid upwards, fisting in my hair and angling my head as he deepened his kiss.

My pussy had been sore earlier, but now it was aching for a different reason. I rubbed against him with purpose, dry humping his cock until I felt my body tightening. Groaning, he pulled me closer, my tits pressed hard against his chest and his hardened length as close to my body as it could get with clothes between us. Pleasure started to pump through my body, only to be interrupted by the sound of my phone ringing. A-fucking-gain.

"No," I whimpered.

Jack released his hold on my hair, reaching out an arm to snag my phone from where I'd dropped it on the cushion next to us.

"She might have been nice about it, but I'm not going to bother because we both know there's only one way you're gonna back off from her and that's when you realize she's already taken. Stay away from what's mine."

I sucked in a breath at the possessiveness evident in his tone, my eyes dropping down to the screen when he swiped his thumb across it to disconnect the call. Only there was one problem. The number on the display wasn't Richard's. The area code wasn't even local. The call had come from Minneapolis. *Minneapolis!*

"No!" I cried out, grabbing the phone from his hand and jumping off his lap.

I paced away from him, pressing the number in my call history to call back.

"Dr. Reed?"

The male voice on the other end of the line sounded confused, understandably so, considering what Jack had told him.

"Yes, this is she. I'm sorry I missed your call just now."

"How odd," he muttered. "There must have been a switch up with the lines or something."

I wasn't about to admit to the true origins of the "or something" in this situation. "To whom am I speaking?"

"Oh, yes. I'm Declan McGowan, head of Pediatrics at Children's Minneapolis. I'm sorry to call you out of the blue like this, but we have an unexpected opening for our Chief of Pediatric Surgery and were hoping you'd consider taking the position. I know it's unorthodox, but considering our current Chief barely beat you out for the position, the board thought we could bypass some of the steps in the hiring process if you were still interested."

My heart pounded wildly in my chest. I'd been crushed when I'd lost the spot as their Chief of Surgery to another candidate last year. It wasn't that I was unhappy with my current job, but this was a big promotion at a well-respected hospital. I swiveled around, my eyes landing on Jack. Dream job, dream man. Different cities. Damn my luck.

Chapter 5

JACK

I couldn't hear the other side of the conversation but I watched closely as Ellison's expression went from surprised to ecstatic. Then she turned to look at me and it shifted once again, this time to indecision. Whatever the person on the line was saying was clearly confusing her and it pissed me off. We were happening. End of story.

I frowned, tempted to take her phone and play a permanent game of "Keep Away." Of course, the doctor in me would never separate her from her connection to the hospital. He would, however, hang up on the fucker making her question our relationship.

She turned away from me, her phone to her ear, and moved to leave the room. Not fucking happening. I snagged her arm and tugged her back into my lap. She scowled at me but gave up struggling to move when she realized I wasn't going to budge.

"Thank you for the opportunity, Declan."

Declan? What kind of a man was named Declan? A man with a pussy, that's who.

"I know you need an answer soon, however my"—she glanced at me— "situation has changed since we last spoke."

I was getting really irritated at being left out of this conversation. I made a grab for her phone so I could listen in but she batted my hand away and pinched the skin so hard I yelped in pain.

"Sorry, one of my patients was just given a shot. Anyway, could I have some time to think it over?"

I growled and ended up with her hand pressed over my mouth again. Think what over, dammit?

"Great. Thank you, Declan. I'll be in touch soon."

She pushed the disconnect button on the phone then smacked my shoulder. "You're such an asshole sometimes, Jack!"

"Who the fuck was that?" I demanded.

She sighed. "Let me have a little time to process, then we'll discuss it, I promise."

I was about to argue, but the feel of her lips on mine and her hot little pussy rubbing against my still hard cock distracted me. She placed little kisses along my jaw until she was by my ear. "Who owns my pussy, honey?"

"You better fucking know who you belong to, Ellie," I snarled as I cupped her ass and yanked her closer, leaving absolutely no room between us. I ripped my shirt from over her head and latched onto a nipple, squeezing her ass hard as I sucked. Removing one hand, I freed my dick from my boxers and shoved the overly large boxers to the side, baring her dripping pussy.

"You're so fucking wet for me, baby. Only for me, right? You're drenched for the man who owns this pussy?" She moaned and I grabbed her hips to slam her down onto my cock as I surged inside of her. One thrust and I was fully seated inside her, her tight, slick walls gripping me, sucking me impossibly deeper.

We both groaned and after the phone calls and her change in attitude after the last one, I had no control left. I drove up into her, bringing her down hard as I entered her over and over, rubbing against her clit every time. My lips licked, bit, and sucked on her large, diamond hard nipples. I loved the way they felt in my mouth, tasted on my tongue.

My hands journeyed from her hips to the firm, round globes of her ass, spreading the cheeks. The middle finger of my right hand ringed her puckered little hole and when she cried out in pleasure, I put the tip inside as I brought her down one last time and we shattered together.

I emptied inside her, long jets of come filling her as I silently cheered my boys on, encouraging them to reach the finish line. I quickly shifted so we were lying on the couch with her trapped below me, staying buried deep inside her. I didn't want any of that shit leaking out. She didn't seem to mind, sighing and wrapping her legs around my waist.

I didn't want to start our relationship off with secrets or dishonesty, so I decided it was time to have the condom conversation, right after I'd buttered her up (go ahead, laugh. I get it) and was still filling her with my cock.

I kissed her deeply first. "Baby, we need to talk," I mumbled against her lips.

"Hmmmm?" her tone was relaxed and mellow. I wasn't above taking advantage of her agreeable mood.

"You know we didn't use condoms last night? Or this morning?"

She groaned, "Shit. Damn you and your giant cock, Jack Halston. I can't think when you're fucking my brains out."

I didn't even try to hide my smug grin.

She rolled her eyes. "You need to figure out how to use a condom, Jack. I swear to all that is holy, if you got me pregnant with your baby, I'm going to kick your ass. Besides, I'd probably be forced to have a C-section because it will inevitably inherit your mammoth ego and a head that large won't fit out of my vagina."

"I'm a doctor, Ellie, I know how to use a fucking condom." I brought my face inches from hers, my expression turning serious. "I just chose not to because I'm going to knock you up, baby. I'm going to fuck you every chance I get until I'm sure my kid is growing in this sexy belly."

Ellison's jaw dropped in shock, and I nodded firmly to emphasize my determination to make this happen.

"And, let's get this out in the open so you can come to terms with it sooner rather than later. If your house isn't up for sale before you find out you're pregnant, you bet your ass I will handle that shit." I softened and kissed her sweetly, "I want you in my bed every night, Ellie. I want to wake up holding you in my arms. And I definitely want to have easy access to the pussy I own."

Her eyes had begun to melt at my words but the last sentence snapped her out of the haze. *Way to go, dipshit.*

She took a deep breath and stared at me, clearly trying to maintain a semblance of calm and control. I was still fully seated inside her and all this talk about babies and having her whenever I wanted had turned my semi-hard erection into stone. I shifted hoping to gain a little relief in another position.

At the movement inside her, Ellison glared at me and tried to push me off of her. Her efforts were futile. I outweighed her by at least a hundred pounds.

"You can't just decide to get me pregnant, Jack!" she exclaimed.

I sealed my mouth over hers before mumbling, "Sure I can," against her lips. Moving with slow, torturous strokes, I drove her out of her fucking mind until she exploded in my arms and I filled her with even more of my seed.

"See?" I murmured.

Our personal stuff would have to wait. We reached the hospital and I confirmed Heather needed additional surgery. I wanted to put my fist through a wall, but my volatile reaction wouldn't help either of us. Ellison pulled me into the scrub room and helped me prep. Her presence soothed my turbulent emotions, infusing me with calm and determination.

"I—I, um … no, you, um," she stuttered, her mind seemingly in a confused and disconnected state.

I pulled out of her, my chest figuratively puffing up at her small sound of protest. Picking her up, she wrapped herself around me like she did when I carried her. I started for my room and the shower, but right when I set her on the counter, my cell phone started ringing.

"Fuck," I muttered. I swiftly stalked across the bedroom to grab it from the dresser. "Dr. Halston," I answered.

"Doctor," Debbie, the shift supervisor said urgently, "Heather developed a complication. The on call doctor wants to open her up again, but I knew you'd want to be the one."

"I'll be there in twenty minutes," I responded before hanging up and tossing my phone on the bed. I rushed into the bathroom and turned the shower on.

"I'm sorry, baby, I've got to go in."

Ellie frowned. "Heather?"

I nodded and hopped into the glass stall. She hurried in after me and began to rush through a shower too. I should have expected she would want to be there as well. Heather was also her patient.

Chapter 6

Ellison

Long hours and exhaustion were the norm in a surgeon's life, but they were hell on relationships. Even when both people were doctors apparently. Jack and I had spent so many hours at the hospital since Heather's emergency surgery that we hadn't been able to revisit the whole 'trying to knock me up' conversation. Not that it had stopped him from giving his pregnancy plan another go or two—or twelve. I'd taken to putting condoms in my purse, lab coat pockets, his pockets, both our cars... pretty much everywhere. Not that it had done a lick of good. In the heat of the moment, I never remembered to ask him to put one on, and he sure as hell never offered. I was beginning to wonder if it was my subconscious trying to tell me I actually wanted the smug bastard to knock me up.

The timing was horrible, though, with the offer of my dream job dropping in my lap. A decision I'd successfully avoided thinking about over the last week, too. Judging by the increasing frequency of the calls coming from Declan, time was running out. The ringing of my phone pulled me out of my thoughts. I glanced down and recognized the number on the display.

Speak of the devil.

"Hey, Declan," I answered. "I'm sorry I haven't been able to get back to you with a response yet."

"No apology needed, Ellison," he assured me. "I expect my call caught you unaware after we went with a different candidate initially."

"It definitely was unexpected," I confirmed.

"The board and I want to make it clear how committed we are to having you on our team."

He was telling me exactly what I would have given almost anything to hear a year ago. "I appreciate that, Declan, and you know how excited I was by the prospect of working for you when I interviewed last year."

"Why do I hear a but in there somewhere?"

"I'm just not sure I want to make the move right now," I sighed.

"Give me a chance to convince you otherwise. Let me take you to lunch so we can talk it through face-to-face."

"Lunch?" I repeated. How would that even work with him in Minneapolis and me in Rock Springs? "When?"

"Today."

His answer shocked me, stopping me in my tracks as I walked through the hospital corridor. "Are you in Nebraska?"

"I told you the board and I wanted to convince you of how serious we are about you taking this job."

"So you hopped on a plane to come to me? For lunch?" I sputtered, feeling flattered by the lengths to which they were willing to go to talk to me about the job. It helped soothe some of the sting from when they'd not selected me for it previously.

"I will if you tell me you're available for lunch today."

My stomach growled, reminding me I'd skipped breakfast. Turning down a free lunch was silly. "Sure, I can do lunch."

"Great! I'll pick you up at the hospital?"

"Sure," I drawled, thinking about how I could make sure we didn't run into Jack while he was here. Not only hadn't we talked about the condom situation, I still hadn't mentioned the job offer either.

"Mmmm," I murmured, savoring the flavor of my bacon wrapped filet. Declan had gone all out, picking me up in a town car and taking me to one of the best steakhouses in town. It was a good thing I didn't have a heavy case load this afternoon, because I could easily see a nap in the sleep room in my near future.

"Smart, successful, gorgeous, and you actually eat real food instead of weeds." Declan's tone was filled with masculine approval.

My eyes popped open in surprise. I'd been enjoying my food so much, I'd kind of forgotten he was there for a minute. I ducked my head in embarrassment and set my fork down on my almost empty plate. Skipping breakfast hadn't been a smart idea since I'd been hungry enough to devour my entire steak in a matter of minutes. "I definitely enjoyed my food," I mumbled.

Declan reached out to grab my hand and squeeze it. I slid my hand away and dropped it onto my lap. *Awkward.*

"I meant it as a compliment, Ellison."

"Thanks," I whispered.

"You done?"

"Yeah," I confirmed, fidgeting in my seat, suddenly aware of how we'd been seated together in a corner booth.

He waved the waiter over, and he cleared the table, leaving the check behind for Declan.

"I've already given you my pitch." And he had, both the last time I'd interviewed and during our lunch. "Not to sound conceited, but I know we have a lot to offer at Children's Minneapolis."

"You do," I replied, nodding in understanding.

"When we spoke last week, you mentioned your situation had changed." His gaze dropped to where my hands were folded in my lap before rising to meet mine again. "I can only assume it's your personal life since our research hadn't indicated anything different in your current position."

"It is." I kept my answer short because I didn't really want to get into it with him.

Declan cocked his head to the side, his gaze speculative as he scanned my face. "I hope you don't mind if I get a little personal with you for a moment."

I waved a hand in a circular motion, giving him permission to continue since I was curious where he was going to take this.

"I'd hate to see you pass up an opportunity like this because of a guy, especially when there will be opportunities for romance in Minneapolis for you."

"Erm..." I sputtered, completely flustered and unsure how to respond.

"Let me be blunt." *Like he wasn't already?* "I didn't see a ring on your finger, so I've got to think this guy probably isn't worth the sacrifice. Not when you can take the job with us and let me take you out on a date after you get settled in up there."

Oh, for criminy's sake. Was I putting off irresistible pheromones or something? First, Richard got all weird when I tried to let him down easily, and then here was Declan trying to lure me into the job in Minneapolis, using himself as bait. Not to mention, Jack doing his best to knock me up.

"That's incredibly kind of you to offer," I murmured, glancing down at my phone as it vibrated in my hand. "And as much as I'd love to discuss this further," —*not*— "they need me back at the hospital."

"They" was really Jack since he was the one trying to reach me. I sent him a quick text, letting him know I was on my way back and chuckled softly at the series of rapid-fire texts which followed.

Jack: I missed you for lunch. You took my favorite meal with you. I had a taste for honey.

Jack: Where did you go?

Jack: Wanna meet me in my office for a quickie?

Jack: I promise to do my best to make you scream, but I'll keep your mouth busy so nobody can hear you.

Me: Poor, starving boy. I'll be there in 5 minutes.

Damn that man! The ride back to the hospital couldn't go fast enough since it was already awkward, and that was before I was blushing wildly and my panties were damp from the images Jack had put in my head. I stayed super quiet, not wanting to do anything to make

Declan think the visible signs of arousal were due to him.

When the car pulled up in front of the hospital, I practically leapt from the vehicle. Unfortunately, Declan followed behind me and insisted on walking me back inside. And my bad luck turned worse as I caught sight of Jack through the glass doors. He didn't give us a chance to make it inside before he stormed through the doors to meet me on the sidewalk and stake his claim.

"Ellie," he growled, his mouth crashing down on mine in a kiss which screamed possessiveness. When he lifted his head, my knees were weak and I was holding on to his arms for dear life.

Declan cleared his throat, drawing my attention to him, right along with Jack's.

"Dr. Jack Halston," he announced, holding his hand out to shake Declan's. "Ellie's fiancé."

Say what now? Had I completely missed his proposal at some point this week?

Declan's gaze dropped to my ringless finger before he chuckled softly. "Dr. Declan McGowan from Children's Minneapolis. I was in town trying to tempt Ellison into joining our team. Considering how things went down last year, I figured a little bit of wooing was in order."

Jack's jaw twitched and he practically growled out his response. "Thanks for treating my girl to lunch, but I've got her from here." I shivered at the hint of sensual threat in his words. I had a feeling he was going to make me pay for not talking to him about the job offer soon.

Chapter 7

JACK

As a doctor, I understood the results of physical violence more than most, but this guy was going to find himself well acquainted with my fist if he didn't get the fuck out of there, fast.

I slipped my arm around Ellison and squeezed her waist, gluing her to my side. Declan (the pussy) was smiling like a cocky son of a bitch, and I glared while Ellison said goodbye and promised to call him. My fingers dug in a little harder, a reflex at the thought of her leaving me and conveying my irritation with her.

She extended her hand and I repressed the need to snatch it back, not wanting even the smallest touch of their skin. Declan finally turned to leave and I kept Ellison beside me as I walked back through the sliding glass doors into the hospital lobby.

"Hey, Dr. Halston, Dr. Reed," greeted a nurse in pink scrubs behind the registration desk. I jerked my chin in response and Ellison gave a weak wave with her free hand. Keeping steady on my path, I headed straight for my office, basically ignoring everyone on the way. Once we reached it, I guided her inside before turning and slamming the door shut. I took a second to calm myself, then turned to face her.

"Care to explain why you're keeping secrets from me and allowing other men to take you out?" I stalked over to her, forcing her to back up, but she only had a few inches before she was pinned between me and the desk. "And, let's be clear about one thing, there is no fucking way you are taking another job and moving away from me. You are mine, Ellison. Or haven't I made that quite obvious by keeping you in my bed every night and doing my damnedest to plant my kid in you?"

Ellison's eyes narrowed and she frowned at me before making an effort to push me away. She might as well be trying to move a block of stone. I wasn't going anywhere until she understood the situation.

"Listen, you big, overbearing caveman," she growled, "you don't make my decisions for me!"

I leaned in until our faces were a breath away. "I think we both know I don't need to. You know you're mine, baby." I grabbed hold of her ass and tugged her body flush against mine. "Or you wouldn't let my bare cock into your honeyed pussy." Lifting her up, I pressed the bulge in my pants into the cradle of her thighs. "Maybe you need a reminder," I rumbled before slamming my mouth down on hers.

"Dr. Reed," a disembodied voice called over the PA system. "You're needed in pediatrics." Fuck! I let her down, making sure she felt the slide of our bodies the whole way.

The page was repeated and I stepped back, giving her room to get around me and leave the office. She shook her head, evidently trying to clear away the thick haze of lust around us. She didn't make eye contact as she headed for the door, so I grabbed her arm forcing her to stop and turn back to me.

"I'll be continuing with my reminder later." Then I planted a quick kiss on her swollen lips and released her.

She pivoted and stepped over the threshold, muttering, "We'll see," and throwing my own words back at me. A grin stole over my face and I shook my head. I fucking loved that woman.

It turned out Ellison had to go into an emergency surgery and I had a scheduled case an hour after she was paged. However, I was still done before her and I hovered around her scrub room, lying in wait, ready to pounce. She finished up and I stayed out of sight until she'd washed and changed back into her street clothes and white lab coat.

I was lounging several feet down the hall and when she saw me, she hesitated for a moment, then lifted her chin stubbornly and continued toward me. It was fucking hot when she got riled and I was about to fan the flame. The thought had my already hard cock fighting like mad to be released and bury itself into her hot, wet pussy.

She began to walk past me without comment. It was adorable how she thought she'd get away with it. I placed a hand between her shoulder blades, the other twisting the knob on the nearest door. Firmly, I steered her through the opening. I shut the door and looked around, realizing we were in a storage closet. I mentally shrugged. It would do.

Ellison was glowering at me, her arms folded across her chest, lifting her breasts, and a hip cocked out.

"Can I help you, Dr. Halston?" she gritted through her teeth. Backing her into the wall, I pressed against her.

"You can scream, Dr. Halston, when I make you come so hard you see fucking stars."

She tried to stifle it, but I heard her little gasp and glanced down to see her nipples hardened into mouthwatering peaks.

"I think you need a cold shower and a craniotomy to remove some of your ego and the Neanderthal inside you," she said with a dismissive air, trying and failing to hide how turned on she was.

"You know you love my cocky caveman." I grinned with smug confidence. "And his big cock."

Before she could protest any further, I gave in to my desperation to claim her, taking her lips in an aggressive kiss. I wanted to overwhelm *her*, but in all reality, love, need, and passion crashed over *me,* too.

Her blouse had buttons down the front and it was easily ripped open, the buttons flying out and pinging off of the shelves. I shoved down the cups of her sexy, pink, lace bra. Her tits spilled out, but were held up by the underwire. It was as though they were being offered up to me, and I took full advantage, sucking on them like they were my favorite candy. They weren't far off anyway.

Ellison moaned, thrusting her tits forward, her hands going to my hair, gripping it to keep me close. Yeah, there was no need, I wasn't going fucking anywhere until I'd accomplished my goal. My mouth still lavishing her tits with attention, I palmed her ass and lifted her so her legs immediately circled my waist. The feeling of her thighs clamping hard almost made me spill right then, but I held back, not wanting to come until I was deep inside her and my boys had a chance to swim their little asses right to her eggs. If I hadn't done so already, this time, I was going to get her good and pregnant.

I dropped her to the ground and flipped positions so I was the one leaning on the wall. My mouth returned to hers and I used my foot to feel around, until it hit something hard. Tearing my mouth away, my hands twisted and plucked at her nipples, while I looked to see and found a large, empty crate on my left. I let Ellison go for a minute to grab a stack of towels and drop them onto the top of the crate. I lowered my zipper and freed my cock. It was so hard, I hissed in pain when the fabric caught. Turning her around, I cupped her tits, massaging them before dragging my hands down to lift the hem of her skirt (thank fuck she wore one that day) and tuck it into her waistband. Then I returned one palm to a big, round tit, the other sliding through her wetness.

"I love how wet you get for me, baby. Fucking drenched."

"Oh, Jack," she moaned.

I carefully descended down to the top of the crate, both arms curling around so they were each on an inner thigh. My legs extended between her legs and I put pressure on them to widen her stance. When she was right where I wanted her, I was staring at the most perfect ass I'd ever seen and eyed the tiny string holding her thong together. It was easy to snap before I used a gentle palm on her back to bend her slightly forward, baring her pink, pussy to me. Her clit was swollen and begging, so I appeased it by sucking it into my mouth.

"Oh, fuck!" Ellie screamed. I knew I should cover her mouth or do something to keep her quiet, but it was the least of my worries. And, I got off on her loud exclamations of pleasure. Licking from top to bottom, I added a finger to mimic what my cock was going to be doing to her soon.

"Mmmmm. I need a honey snack," I purred. "My snack only, right, Ellie?" I asked with a little more force. When she didn't answer right away, I pinched her clit while my tongue plunged inside her.

"Yes!" she cried out.

"Good girl. Who owns this pussy, baby?"

"You," she panted. I wanted to ask her if she loved me but I chickened out and brought her to a screaming orgasm instead.

Gripping her hips, I widened my own legs to keep her open as I guided her down enough to line my cock up and then slammed her down onto it. We both gasped at the feel of being joined together so intimately. With her position keeping her wide, I bent my knees and they came up enough so she could lean forward and rest against them. It bared her spectacular ass again and the flesh begged to be spanked. A sharp crack rang through the sound of our panting and otherwise quiet closet.

Ellie jerked and it seated me even deeper.

"Oh, fuck yes, baby!" I cried out.

I wrapped my fingers around the edges of the crate, and used the pressure of my feet on the floor for leverage, and began to thrust up hard enough to bounce her body and make it slam back down each time. Ellie sat up straight and squeezed the fuck out of my dick every time she landed.

"Yes, yes, yes," she chanted, adding a "harder, Jack!" in there for good measure.

I put every bit of my strength into fucking her. When I felt the telling clenching of her walls, I kept a tight grip on her body, her back tight against my front, and pushed to my feet. Turning, I growled, "Grab the shelf, baby. Don't let go."

Once her hands were secure, I wrapped her legs backwards around my hips, then drove into her, gaining speed every time she cried out until I was fucking her with frenzy. I had no rhythm, no finesse, it was raw, animalistic fucking.

She screamed my name as her body shuddered, her pussy strangling my cock, sucking it in as I thrust three more times before exploding. I pushed against her and with her legs so high up, I was in a good position to seal our groins together, holding myself inside so it would be as deep as possible as I shot my load and kept any from leaking out.

Finally, we both lost the strength to hold our position and I slipped out of her, letting her feet down as I did. She mewled in protest and mentally, my chest swelled with pride at satisfying my woman. I held her against me, leaning my head so my mouth was at her ear.

"Was that a sufficient reminder, Ellie?" My hands slid down her soft skin to splay over her belly. "This time, I know I gave you my baby. You are mine Ellie, you and our babies."

Ellie jerked at my words. "Babies? As in, plural?"

I nuzzled her neck, "At least four. I want lots of little Ellies running around.

"*At least* four?" she exclaimed. "When the fuck am I going to have time to raise four kids and be a doctor?"

I kissed her ear. "I have no doubt you could handle it baby. You're the strongest woman I've ever met." Even though the words were one hundred percent true, I smiled in triumph as I felt her melt a little. "And, I'll be there to help you every step of the way."

She snorted and I turned her around to face me, frowning and hurt. "You don't believe I'll be a good dad?"

She looked chagrined. "No, Jack. I'm sorry. I think you'll be an amazing dad, but four kids with two doctors for parents? I can't help wondering if you're banking on me wanting to quit and stay home with our kids."

I scowled, but realized how easy it would be for her to come to this conclusion and softened my expression. "I never considered taking away your career, Ellie. It's part of you just like it is me. You're an amazing doctor. I hope you trust me enough to believe me."

She gave me a small smile, but I could tell she wasn't entirely convinced. The only thing I could do was prove it. I had the rest of our lives to do it, so I pushed it away for another day.

Chapter 8

Ellison

"We need to stop over at Wyatt and Bailey's house on our way home."

My eyebrows practically climbed all the way up to my hairline at the casual way Jack tossed his comment out, as though it wasn't a big deal. Today had already been interesting with Jack's reaction to my lunch with Declan. Meeting part of his family would just cap the day off, especially since I'd been looking forward to changing out of my work clothes and pouring myself a big glass of wine. Annoyed, I grumbled under my breath, "I know you've been working all day and you're stuck in scrubs instead of the kickass outfit you put on this morning because I ruined your blouse when I ripped it from your body, but I'm sure my family will love you anyway." I mimicked what I wished he would have said.

"I promise it won't take long, and you look hot as fuck in those scrubs, just like you do in anything you wear." Apparently, I hadn't been quiet enough. *Whoopsie.* "My nephew, Jack, has been running a fever all day and my sister wants me to stop by to make sure it's nothing serious."

Oh, no! I felt guilty for being such a grump. "Of course we should go."

"He usually eats like a little pig, but Bailey said he's barely eating and incredibly irritable. Plus, he's been rubbing his ear a lot today. It's probably nothing more than teething his first tooth, but she wants to rule out other possible causes like an ear infection and couldn't get them in to see the twins' pediatrician until tomorrow afternoon."

"Poor baby," I sighed, turning towards him and offering a commiserating smile. "But it's nice that Uncle Jack can race to the rescue."

He reached over and gave my thigh a quick squeeze as he pulled into the driveway. "If it's nice for Jack and Julia to have a surgeon for their uncle, imagine how lucky our kids will be to have two surgeons for their mom and dad."

Our kids. How was it possible we were both calling them that already? My hand drifted down to my stomach, and I tried to imagine what it would be like if I were pregnant with his baby. Neither of us had used the L-word yet and I'd been offered my dream job in another state. The timing wouldn't be good for a baby, at all.

And then we walked into his sister's house, and my biological clock roared to life. I'd always thought Jack was handsome, but seeing him with his baby niece and nephew made him even more irresistible. There really wasn't anything like a sexy man with a baby in his arms to make your ovaries feel like they were about to explode. Sneaky bastard, if baby Jack hadn't been sick, I would have been positive he'd planned our visit for precisely this reason.

"I'm so happy to finally meet you," Bailey whispered to me as we both watched from the doorway while Jack checked his namesake over. Or I looked on while she stared at me appraisingly until I felt a blush creep up my cheeks.

"Finally? Jack and I haven't been a couple very long."

She chuckled softly. "Maybe not, but I've been hearing your name pop up in conversation with my brother more and more over the last six months."

I tore my attention away from the sight of Jack with a look of pure adoration on his face as he stared down at the adorable baby boy in his arms, one long finger rubbing along his gums. It wasn't easy, but I was intrigued by what Bailey had just said. "Really?" She nodded, and I lowered my voice before continuing the conversation. "When did Jack first mention me?"

Bailey cocked her head to the side and tapped her bottom lip with a finger. "It's been at least a year because I feel like I was pregnant enough to just be in maternity clothes and the babies are seven months old."

"Huh," I murmured, my gaze flitting back to Jack. "I'm surprised it was that long ago. We didn't know each other very well back then."

"It wasn't what he said but how he said it," she explained. "You were working a case together and his eyes lit up when he mentioned your role in helping to save the patient. The way he looked when he said your name, combined with how complimentary he was about your surgical skills put you on my sisterly radar."

"He's not exactly known around the hospital for offering praise to other doctors."

Bailey's soft chuckle turned into a belly laugh, drawing Jack's gaze our way. "This doesn't surprise me. I love my brother dearly, but he can be a bit arrogant. Remind me to tell you the story of how he reacted to Wyatt's and my relationship some time."

Jack glared at his sister before looking back down at the baby in his arms. "Your mommy is being a brat, buddy. But it's a good thing, because she reminded me that you and I need to have a talk about what it means to be a big brother." He stood up and walked over to the crib decorated in pink where Julia slept peacefully.

"See your sister down there?" He leaned over so he and the baby could look at Julia. "Your toughest responsibility as her big brother is going to be to protect her from all the boys out there. You'll have a lot of help from your daddy and me, but there will be times when you're the only line of defense. Doesn't matter if the boy is your friend or not, a good guy or a bad one—you'll know he isn't good enough for Julia. None of them will be."

"Oh, for goodness sakes, Jack," Bailey huffed as she walked over to take her son from his arms. "He's too young to understand a single word you're saying."

"Hey, you can't blame me for giving him a head start." He threw his arms up defensively. "I just want to make up for the late one I got."

The look that passed between brother and sister brought tears to my eyes—Bailey's too.

She settled baby Jack into his crib before moving back to give her brother a hug. "You better not make me cry or Wyatt will try to kick your ass," she mumbled into his shirt.

"Nah," Jack answered. "He'll forgive me when I tell him his baby boy is about to get his first tooth and doesn't need to see the doctor tomorrow."

"What a relief," Bailey sighed, leaning back and beaming up at him.

"Besides, it's not like he could kick my ass anyway," Jack drawled, dropping a kiss on her head. "And we won't be here when he gets home."

He crossed the room, pulling me to his side and whispering in my ear. "We need to get home so I can make sure my reminder from this afternoon stuck, and give my swimmers another chance in case they didn't do their job earlier."

Jack didn't get any arguments from me. If I'd been wearing panties under my scrub pants, they would have been drenched.

Life with Jack moved lightning fast. One week we're work colleagues who flirt and the next we're friends who are practically joined at the hip. In one night, we moved from being firmly in the friend zone to an exclusive relationship. Then, I felt my biological clock ticking and the next week my period was late. It always came every twenty-eight days, like clockwork, and should have started two days ago. There was no sign of it starting anytime soon. I was pretty sure Jack had gotten his wish and knocked me up, which is how I found myself hiding in his bathroom first thing this morning while he was making breakfast. I'd peed on the stick three minutes ago and was trying to get up the nerves to look at the results.

"You can do this," I murmured softly. "No matter what the test says, you're a strong woman and you'll figure out the right thing to do."

My little pep talk wasn't doing anything to stop the flutter of butterflies in my belly. Taking a deep breath, I picked up the stick from the bathroom counter and flipped it over.

Not pregnant.

The air left my lungs with a heaving sigh. The emotion I should have felt was relief since I wasn't sure I was ready for babies, let alone to have them with Jack. Although I'd known him through work for two years, we'd only really been a couple for two weeks. Plus, I still needed to decide what to do about the job offer from Children's Minneapolis. My brain knew this was probably for the best, but it seemed my heart had a different perspective because I felt like it was breaking.

Logic didn't factor into what I was feeling. I'd spent the last two days thinking maybe he'd been right and he'd gotten me pregnant. *How was I going to tell him I wasn't?* He didn't even know my period was late because I hadn't been ready to talk to him about the real possibility of me being pregnant. It seemed like the right decision at the time, but I wished I'd said something because then I wouldn't be facing this alone. Sitting on the side of the tub, sobbing into my hands, I came to a few realizations.

I loved Jack Halston.

I couldn't take the job in Minneapolis.

And I wanted to have his babies, all four of them.

My tears shifted into a chuckle snort at the irony. Back in my undergrad years, I'd been a little judgy towards the girls who were there for their "Mrs. Degree," but I was going to turn down a promotion because of a man. Not just any man, though. I had a feeling my fellow nerd girls would make the same decision if given a chance with Dr. Jack Halston. Too bad for them he was all mine.

Chapter 9

JACK

I placed a bowl of strawberries on a tray along with pancakes, syrup, and orange juice. I wanted to make sure my woman had a good breakfast because I had plans to wear her the fuck out today. It was rare for us to have a day where we were both off and I intended to spend it in bed.

Lifting the tray, I carefully walked to the bedroom and was surprised to see the bed empty. There was light coming from the bathroom door, so I set the tray on the dresser and padded over to the closed door. I turned the knob, and as it opened, I heard soft crying. Alarmed, I raced the rest of the way inside to see Ellison sitting on the edge of the tub, her elbows on her knees, her face buried in her hands.

I scooped her up and took her seat, settling her on my lap, tucking her head under my chin, then rubbing her back in slow circles.

"What's wrong, baby?"

She sniffled for another minute before lifting her head, her brown eyes watery with tears.

"I didn't think I wanted it," she whispered as more tears tracked down her cheeks.

I gently wiped them away with my thumb. "Wanted what?"

"The life you were planning for us, the one with four kids, two surgeons, one house, and a partridge in a pear tree."

Her words sounded wistful and I took it as a good sign. "Baby, I'd really prefer a dog, but if this is your way of telling me you're pregnant, we can have whatever fucking pets you want."

She began to cry in earnest, burying her face into my chest. I started to panic and wonder if I'd gotten it wrong. If she was trying to tell me she had decided to take the job in Minneapolis, I'd chain her to my bed until I convinced her she didn't belong anywhere but here with me. I knew her, though. No matter the amount of time we'd been together, she was a part of me and I had no doubt that we wanted the same future. It was up to me to make her see it.

My eyes suddenly caught sight of a white, plastic stick sitting on the counter.

Still holding Ellie close, I reached out one long arm and picked up the pregnancy test. I stared at it from the back for a moment, a little nervous. Are you sure you aren't the one with the vagina, dude?

Holding my breath, I flipped it over and the air came whooshing out in a rush.

Not Pregnant.

Chained to the bed it is.

I stood with her cradled in my arms and tossed the test into the garbage. Taking her to the bed, I lay her down and covered her body with mine.

"I told you before, Ellie. You're mine. I won't let you leave me. If you want to wait to start a family, I'll give you whatever you ask, except let you go. I love you and I know you love me. We were meant to be together and I'm going to keep you right here until I've convinced you it's true."

Her chocolate brown eyes widened as she stared into my face. "You—you love me?" she stuttered.

It dawned on me that I've laid myself bare to her, opened up my chest and gave her the ammunition to rip my heart out. Not for one second did I regret it, though. She was worth it. She was everything.

I brushed my lips over hers then leaned back to gaze at her beautiful face. "Yeah, Ellie. I love you. I'm sure I've loved you since the moment I first met you. It took me a while to realize you were everything I never knew I always wanted. Once I understood my feelings, I decided there was no other recourse but to make you mine. I know you love me, Ellie." I took a shuddering breath and made the last step into complete vulnerability. "Right?"

She glided her hands up my chest and neck until she was cupping my face. "I love you more than anything in this world, Jack. You're right, you own me. And, I don't want to wait. I want to have a family with you, now."

The relief I felt was overwhelmingly acute. Obviously I'd been more nervous than I'd thought. I grinned at her and melded our mouths together, pouring all of my love into the kiss.

I pulled back and stared at the gorgeous woman beneath me and noticed the dried tears on her face. After another quick kiss, I caressed her cheek, tracing the salty tracks. "No need to cry, baby. I'll fuck you as many times as I need to until you're swollen with my baby in your belly," I promised and was rewarded with the sweet sound of her laughter.

A thought crashed into me and I jumped from the bed and started for the door, halting after a few steps and whirling around. I pointed at her. "You. Stay."

She scrunched her cute little nose in distaste. "You better be practicing for when we have a dog, Dr. Halston."

I groaned helplessly. Whenever she called me Dr. Halston, it turned me the fuck on. I pointed to her once again and raced from the room, determined to get back as fast as possible. I practically flew down the back set of stairs to my office and snatched a small blue box from the drawer of my desk. Just as swiftly, I returned to our room and climbed back over her.

Satisfied she'd stayed where I put her, I kissed her forehead. "Good girl." She glared at me.

I put the most innocent expression on my face that I could manage. "I guess you don't want your treat for being obedient then?" I held up the petite box and her jaw dropped, an excited sparkle in her eye. "Did you think I was fucking around when I told the pussy I was your fiancé?" I grinned, remembering how I'd staked my fucking claim on my woman.

"You never said anything, I assumed—"

I cut her off, "Well, you were wrong. I was trying to think of a romantic way to propose, something incredibly romantic. But, I can't wait any longer. I need everyone to know you're not available. I own you."

She rolled her eyes, but there was a smile playing around the corners of her mouth. I untied the silky, white bow and removed the lid. Taking out a black, velvet box, I flipped it open to reveal a five-carat, cushion cut diamond, set in a diamond encrusted, platinum band. Ellie gasped, her face filled with awe as she touched the ring with the tips of her fingers, tracing it in the velvet display.

"It's stunning, Jack. I love it."

"You love who?" I asked gruffly, jealous of a stupid ring.

She winked at me. "I love you." Then I heard her mutter under her breath, "Almost as much."

"You're going to pay for that, baby," I grumbled. Taking the ring from the box, I slid it onto her trembling finger. "You know what this mean, right?" I asked warily, and then it occurred to me we hadn't discussed her ridiculous job offer. "No moving, no new job, no Declan," I spat his name, still fighting the urge to rearrange his face for trying to steal my girl.

Ellison huffed, "Do you have to steamroll everything?"

I frowned, offended at her accusation and a tad unsure what she meant. "No," I said with conviction. "But when my fiancée is considering moving out of state and"—I glared fiercely at her—"lets other men take her to lunch, I'm sure as fuck going to steamroll anything or anyone who gets in my way."

Her lips turned down into a pout, adorable and utterly irresistible. I drank from her lips until she bit my lip a little harder than usual.

"Fuck! What the hell, Ellie?"

"You distracted me."

"And?" I asked with a single raised eyebrow.

She scowled and it grew when I couldn't keep myself from grinning. I fucking loved her to pieces.

"I was going to tell you I'd decided not to take the job. I want to stay here, to be with you. But your damn caveman tactics stole my thunder. I wanted to tell you I was devastated not to be pregnant. I love you, Neanderthal and all."

I winked at her and smiled. "I'll make it up to you," I vowed before kissing her until she was breathless and quaking with need.

There was only one thing left to do before I could spend the rest of the day making her scream my name. Tearing my mouth from hers (no easy feat, I might add), I stretched over to grab her cell phone off of the nightstand.

"Call him, now," I demanded, handing her the phone.

She was watching me with amusement. "Call who?"

"Don't mess with me, baby. You've already guaranteed I'm going to punish you by making you orgasm as hard and as often as possible until you pass out. If you want to keep it up, you'll earn a round two."

She winked. "Promise?"

I laughed, but grabbed the phone away from her and looked for his contact info, pressing send before putting it on speaker. She made a grab for it, but I caught her wrists and held them locked in one hand above her head.

"Ellie!" Douche bag's voice came over the line and my hand tightened at the use of her nickname. My nickname. I opened my mouth to tell him off, but Ellison started talking.

"Declan," she replied.

"I hope you're calling to accept the job, and give me a chance."

This guy was pissing me off more and more. I could feel the flush of anger and knew my face had to be turning red.

"Um," Ellie was giving me a warning in her eyes, telling me to back off and let her handle it. I nodded jerkily, willing to acquiesce to her request, for the moment.

"No, I am incredibly flattered and it's certainly a very tempting offer." I growled at the idea she might find it tempting to leave me.

She hissed at me to shut up, quiet enough so it wouldn't carry into the phone.

"Please, Ellie. Give us a chanc—"

I'd had it. "Her name is Dr. Reed or soon to be Dr. Halston, whichever of those you prefer to call her," I snapped. "Actually, you won't be calling her anything. So back the fuck off and leave my woman alone."

I hit the disconnect button and dropped the phone onto the plush, carpeted floor. I didn't give her an opportunity to lash out at me. I busied myself with giving her six screaming orgasms until she passed out.

If possible, I was even more determined to knock my woman up. Alright boys, we're going to war.

Chapter 10

Ellison

Jack had been doing his best to turn that negative pregnancy test positive over the last few days, waking me up at least once every night to give it an extra try. He'd turned me into a walking zombie with all his attempts. I hadn't been this tired since my residency years. I used to be able to go for several days on very little sleep, but it looked like hitting my thirties meant I was too old to pull all-nighters anymore, even for sex.

I buried my face in my pillow when I felt the slide of the sheet on the bare skin of my back. "Must sleep."

My words were muffled but apparently clear enough for Jack to understand based on his deep chuckle. "Up and at 'em, baby. You've got things to do before I leave for my shift at the hospital."

"No," I moaned. "I really don't have anything I need to do."

"Are you sure about that?"

"Yeah," I confirmed. "I'm pretty sure we did all the things already last night. And super early this morning. As much as I love you and as hot as you are, I don't think I can handle any more orgasms until I get some sleep."

"I'm not talking about sex, Ellie."

He wasn't? That was certainly a surprise. I raised up on an elbow to look at him and practically fell over at the sight of what he was holding in his hand. "You know you're crazy, right?"

He waived the little white stick in my face. "You love my brand of crazy."

"I just took one three days ago, and it was negative," I grumbled, slumping back down on the mattress.

He shrugged his shoulders. "Maybe you peed on it wrong."

"I did no such thing!" I huffed. "I'm a board certified pediatric surgeon. Peeing on a stick isn't past my skill set."

"And yet your period is almost a week late, you're exhausted, and you shoved me off the bed last night when I tried to play with your tits," he quipped. "Something which would usually make you cream your panties."

"But the test was negative," I repeated.

He gripped my hands and tugged me from the bed, nudging me towards the bathroom. "As you so kindly pointed out already, you're a board certified surgeon. You should be familiar with the notion of false negatives."

"Do you really think that's what it was?" I whispered as I crossed through the doorway. As odd as it sounded, the possibility hadn't even crossed my mind. I'd been too upset to consider it.

"Only one way to find out," he replied.

I hiked up his shirt, the one I'd tugged on when he'd finally let me fall back asleep last night, and squatted down to sit on the toilet. "Out!" I ordered him.

"C'mon," he groused. "I want to be here every step of the way with you. We're in this together."

"The only way you're going to be in the bathroom during the peeing on the stick step is if the day ever comes when you're the one doing the peeing."

"Fine," he huffed before stepping out and closing the door behind him. He didn't give me long, though. As soon as I'd finished peeing and flushed, the door swung open again. He gave me just enough time to wash my hands, while he was busy wrapping the test in a washcloth, before he picked me up and carried me back to bed. Laying me gently down on the mattress, he quickly followed and looked at me with boyish delight in his eyes. "Is it time yet?"

"Not yet," I giggled. "You have to wait a couple more minutes."

"I guess I'd better find a way to pass the time," he murmured against my mouth, claiming them in a quick but deep kiss before trailing his lips lower. Along my jaw, down my neck, teasing the sides of my tits. He made it to my belly before he spoke again, whispering softly, "I think it's time to prove to your mommy that you're in there."

My breath caught in my throat at the sight of his dark head against my pale skin. "Please, please, please," I chanted as he reached for the washcloth and carefully lifted a corner to peek inside. The blinding smile which spread across his face gave me my answer before he could show me the test. It was positive. It had to be. I leaned over, bumping his shoulder to make room for me, and looked down at the digital screen.

Pregnant.

"We're pregnant."

"Damn straight you are," he confirmed, tossing the stick and washcloth to the floor and diving on top of me. "And now we need to celebrate."

If I'd been wearing them, my panties would have melted at his happiness. "How exactly do you plan to celebrate this news when you need to be at the hospital soon?"

His smile turned into a sly grin. "I've got an hour."

My head swiveled so I could peer at the clock on the bedside table. "No, you don't. You need to leave in like ten minutes."

"I set the clock ahead before I woke you up," he informed me, tugging my shirt over my head. "I wanted to make sure we had enough time to celebrate before I had to go."

"You were that confident?"

He tore his shirt off and shoved his boxers down his legs. "There wasn't a doubt in my mind, Ellie."

"How about you show me how you planned to spend that hour?"

He dropped a quick kiss to my belly and then settled in between my legs. "You're so fucking beautiful, baby," he murmured against the sensitive skin of my inner thigh. His breath was hot against my naked flesh as his tongue flicked out for a quick lick. "And I'm addicted to the taste of your honey."

That's all it took for me to suddenly be on the edge of a climax. He'd barely touched me, but that didn't stop my walls from clenching against his tongue when he slid it inside my pussy. His finger circled my clit, and I felt myself lose control. He moaned against my pussy, and vibrations were enough to send me flying over the edge. My legs shook as they tightened around his head while I came.

"I'll never grow tired of hearing your cries while I eat your pussy," he growled before he levered up onto his knees and pulled my hips until I shifted lower on the bed. Then he impaled me with one hard thrust. "But there's nothing better than the feeling of your wet pussy wrapped tightly around my cock, knowing my baby is growing inside your belly."

He began moving hard and fast, going deep with each powerful thrust but holding my hips gently all the while. Over and over again, with his eyes locked on mine the whole time. Sex with Jack had always been amazing, from the very first time, but this time was different. Better.

More. His ring was on my finger, and I was pregnant with his baby. His eyes were filled with lust, but it was tempered by love. So much love.

His strokes triggered a tingling in my spine, making my toes clench against the sheets. Then it hit me, a climax bigger than I'd ever felt before, making me scream his name until my voice was hoarse. He kept going, hammering into me until I'd come again and my legs felt like jelly. When I didn't think I could take any more, he planted himself deep one more time and groaned. His cock jerked, and the heat from his semen sparked another orgasm for me.

"You were made for me," he murmured as he pulled me tight. "I should have admitted it to myself two years ago. If I had, then you'd be pregnant with our second or third child by now."

Resting my head against his chest, I laughed softly. "It's hard to know what would have happened if either of us had made a move back then, but I love that we had two years to get to know each other the way we did."

"You're happy about the baby, then?" he asked, a hint of vulnerability in his tone.

"I'm so happy." Three little words but they held a depth of meaning, intended to clear away the doubt I'd instilled within this amazing man who loved me.

"Happy enough to marry me tomorrow?"

I laughed, thinking he was joking until I caught the look of utter seriousness on his face. I had no doubt he'd find a way for us to exchange our vows tomorrow if I agreed, but I didn't hesitate to give him my answer. "Yes, honey."

Epilogue

JACK

I gently placed my infant son in his crib, running a hand through his soft, feathery hair. Eric was a quiet baby and was already sleeping through the night. Turning on the monitor, I went into the hall and pulled the door so it was almost shut. I'd already tucked in my sweet little two-year-old, Addy, so I padded down the hall to the den where my beautiful wife was stretched out on the couch, watching a movie. Making a beeline for her, I lowered myself down so my body covered hers.

"I do believe both of our kids are asleep, Dr. Halston," I whispered as I began to nibble on her ear. "Whatever will we do with this time alone?"

Ellie tilted her head back, giving me more access to her neck, and I placed hot, wet, open-mouthed kisses down to the valley between her tits. She was wearing a loose tank and the neckline gaped so I hooked a finger in the fabric and tugged it down. I groaned at the sight of her naked tits, fuller from two kids and nursing our son. I licked around one before taking it into my mouth.

I bit the tip lightly and she gasped, every muscle in her body freezing, before she started shaking. I lifted my head, surprised she'd come so fast. However, her face wasn't lost in ecstasy. Nope, she was laughing, her mouth pinched as she tried to keep quiet.

"If I wasn't so secure in my ability to make you come, this could be a pretty big blow to my ego, baby."

She snickered and pointed behind me. "What were you saying about the kids being asleep?"

I levered myself up onto my elbows and twisted to look back.

A pillow was floating through the door, or at least, it looked as though it was. Really, it had two little feet, just barely visible underneath the large pillow. Small, delicate fingers grasped the edges and it was moving slowly, hesitantly.

I smiled in exasperated amusement. Addy had reached the stage where she was like an ostrich sticking their head in the sand. She seemed to believe if she couldn't see us, we couldn't see her.

"Addy," I said sternly. The pillow jerked and lowered, revealing her big brown eyes. They were open wide, shocked at having been discovered. It was adorable as fuck. My kids were the cutest, I didn't care what Wyatt said. I loved my nieces and nephews, but come on, my daughter was a fucking knockout.

"Back to bed, sneaky."

Her wide chocolate eyes filled with tears and I looked at Ellie frantically. She raised a brow and stared at me challengingly. *Shit.* I forgot about our bet. Ellie was convinced I couldn't hold firm with my baby girl when she cried. It was ridiculous. I was man enough to deal with her tears without caving.

I narrowed my eyes and glared at her, my heart starting to crack with the little sniffles coming from behind me. I took a deep breath and steeled myself against the overwhelming desire to scoop her up and give her anything and everything she wanted.

Pulling up Ellie's shirt, I climbed off of her and faced my Addy, crumbling at the sight of the big, fat tears rolling down her face. I swiftly moved to her and scooped her up in my embrace. Her small arms wound around my neck and she rested her head against my chest, her head tucked under my chin.

"Monsters, Daddy," she hiccupped. "I want to seep wif you and Mommy." My resolve was fast disappearing, then she played the trump card. "I'm scared." It was my job to protect my baby girl, to scare away the monsters, to be her hero, damn it.

"Sure, baby girl."

Ellie cleared her throat noisily and I glanced back to see her shaking her head. I threw her a pleading look but she had no sympathy, snickering at me again. *Callous, unfeeling woman!*

She finally stood and walked over to us. "You should sleep in your big girl bed, Addy. Daddy will check for monsters, then you go to sleep, okay?" She rubbed Addy's back in slow circles as she spoke.

Addy leaned back and looked up at me with soft, sad eyes. "Pwease, Daddy?" *Well, fuck.*

Ellie could obviously see I was about to give in and she shrugged before turning and muttering under her breath as she passed me. "Sucker."

I couldn't hide behind the pillow anymore. She was right, I was a complete sucker for my kids.

"I guess I'll have to wear something else to bed since ours will be so crowded," she called after she disappeared around the corner.

I quickly followed after her. "Something else?"

She glanced back with a smug smile. "Well, not so much something else as plain old something instead of nothing at all."

I hurried down the hall and into my daughter's bedroom, Ellie's laughter trailing behind me. Holding Addy, we checked the closet, under the bed, and every nook and crevice for monsters.

"See, baby girl? Nothing to be afraid of," I crooned, kissing her forehead. I bent to lay her in her new toddler, princess bed, but she clung tightly to me.

"Stay, Daddy?" she begged, tugging at my heartstrings. However, it had been a week since Ellie and I had an early night like this, one where we both weren't too tired for more than a quick fuck. I was dying to make love to my wife, to worship every inch of her delectable body, to taste her honey.

"Can you be my best girl, Addy? Show me how brave you are?" Her eyes teared up again and I swore a violent streak of curses for the shit I was going to take from Ellie for what I was about to do. Not to mention the shit from Bailey, Wyatt, and my dad, because Ellie would be on the phone first thing when she found out. My dick didn't give a fuck, so I gave up trying. "If you go right to sleep and be brave, you can have some of your birthday cake for breakfast."

Her eyes got wide, suddenly dry with no evidence of tears, and a smile spread over her sweet face as she nodded vigorously.

"Okay," I said as I tucked her in. "The faster you go to sleep, the faster morning will be here and you can have cake."

She immediately scrunched her eyes shut and snuggled into the teddy bear I placed in her arms. When she was settled, I raced to my bedroom, halting in disappointment when my wife wasn't waiting naked in bed for me.

Then I noticed the trail of clothes on the floor leading to the bathroom. When I opened the door, I stopped to admire the view of Ellie standing in the shower under the hot spray of water, cascading down her incredible body.

I shed my clothes at lightning speed and stepped in behind her, pulling her back against me and cupping her full tits. I fucking loved her body and it only got more luscious and beautiful with every baby.

"You promised her cake, didn't you?" she asked.

I ignored her and slipped a hand down to play with her pussy, making her moan. I was so fucking hard, I was afraid it would only take one shift of her hips to make me explode. But, I wanted a taste first.

I dropped to my knees and turned her so I was at eye level with her pretty pussy. "I've missed your honey, baby." A long, slow lick had her shuddering with need. I ate her pussy, savoring every bite, lick, and suck. I made her come twice before I was satisfied and surged to my feet, lifting her off the ground and impaling her as I pressed her against the wall.

"Oh fuck! You feel so good, baby."

She squeezed her inner muscles and I was on the verge of coming, so I began to pump into her, while I played with her clit. She was crying out and meeting my every thrust with her hips.

"You ready, baby? I'm going to come, Ellie! Fuck, I need you to come!"

Suddenly, she froze and I reared back in surprise.

"Condom, Jack," she panted.

I scowled. "Fuck the condom, Ellie. I only take you bare."

She mirrored my dark expression and opened her mouth to argue, but I didn't let her get a word out before covering her mouth with my own and driving in two more times, setting us both off.

After we had Addy, I'd agreed to wear a condom until Ellie was ready to try again, but the first time I tried it, I couldn't feel her and I pulled out, tore it off, and dove back inside. She was pretty pissed when she turned up pregnant three months later. I thought it was fucking fantastic and I told her so. She accused me of being a Neanderthal and stormed out of the room. With a little chocolate and a whole lot of eating her pussy, it didn't take me long to convince her to forgive me.

"Dad!" Addy yelled, banging on our bedroom door. "I know you're in there!"

I lifted my mouth from where I was devouring Ellie's honey and frowned. "Adult time, Addy!" I shouted, grateful I remembered to lock the door.

Ellie chortled and I glared at her.

"Why do I have to watch the other kids?" she whined.

"Because I said so. Now, go be a good daughter and give your mom and I some alone time."

She stomped away from the door, muttering loudly, "You better not be giving me another brother or sister!"

Ellie was all out laughing and I scowled. She held her hands up in a sign of surrender. "Hey, you're the one who decided five was the magic number."

The dark look on my face must have morphed into complete and utter shock because Ellie rolled her eyes and gave me a dry look.

"Five?" I croaked.

"Yup. What did you think would happen when you couldn't keep a rubber on your giant cock?"

I tried, I really did, but every time I felt something between us, I couldn't stand it. It was like I couldn't breathe until we were one.

After a moment the shock wore off and a smug smile crossed my face. I looked down at her currently flat stomach. *Way to go, boys*.

Books By This Author

Risqué Contracts Series

Penalty Clause

Contingency Plan

Fraternization Rule

Yeah, Baby Series

Baby, You're Mine

Baby Steps

Baby, Come Back

About the Author

Hello! My name is Fiona Davenport and I'm a smutoholic. I've been reading raunchy romance novels since... well, forever and a day ago it seems. And now I get to write sexy stories and share them with others who are like me and enjoy their books on the steamier side. Fiona Davenport is my super-secret alias, which is kind of awesome since I've always wanted one.

You can connect with me online on Facebook or Twitter.

Made in the USA
Coppell, TX
20 March 2022